ABOUT THIS BOOK

The illustrations for this book were done in acryla gouache on Borden & Riley Paris paper and finished in digital line. This book was edited by Andrea Spooner and designed by Véronique Lefèvre Sweet. The production was supervised by Bernadette Flinn, and the production editors were Annie McDonnell and Esther Reisberg. The text was set in Charcuterie Serif, and the display type is the artist's hand lettering.

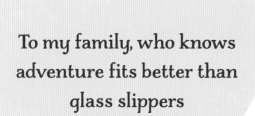

To my family, who knows adventure fits better than glass slippers

Cinda Meets Ella
a fairly queer tale

by WALLACE West

Little, Brown and Company
New York Boston

The only thing Cinda loved more than jalapeño fritters was adventure.

Her parents agreed.

Too bad they were gobbled by a gator while adventuring.
But Cinda's critters helped her through that
heck of a hard time.

Then Cinda's aunt Hildy barged in, announcing
she was in charge (of *EVERYTHING*).

"You need adult supervision," said Hildy. "And acceptable clothes."

"And another room," said her two boys.

"And to say bye to those *animals*," said Hildy .

"We're allergic," coughed the boys.

After Hildy crated up the critters and crammed
her into a dress, Cinda was nothin' but miserable.

Until someone as striking as a sunset rode up.
They were wearing a getup Hildy would hate.
Cinda loved it. "Howdy," said The Rider,
tossing Cinda a card.

Aunt Hildy snatched it like a vulture pecking bones.

Contest at the DEL REINA
RANCHO
hosted by
Ella DEL Reina
LASSO! RACE!
Surprise Challenge!
$$$
Winner of **2** outta **3**
Gets a $$$ Prize.

Hope flared inside Cinda. She could
use that prize money to buy her critters
back and get them a barn far from Hildy
and her coughing cousins.

"The Del Reinas are the richest family this side of
Kingsville," said Hildy to the boys. "If one of you wins,
Ella will be so impressed, she'll *marry* you!"

The Rider said, "Ain't they young for wedding cake?"

"Never too early for true love," said Hildy.

"Anyone can compete?" asked Cinda, grinning big as a bayou.

"Anyone." The Rider winked. "'Specially you," they said before galloping away.

The next day, Hildy locked up Cinda and hightailed it to the Rancho Del Reina with the boys (and every last string of lassoing rope).

Cinda was trying to wrangle her way out the window when a boar bigger than a boulder trotted up.

"I'm Merrie Hoggmüther," the boar snorted. "Promised your parents I'd check in on you if their adventuring ended."

"Well, howdy! I sure could use your hoof getting outta here," said Cinda.

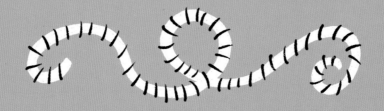

Cinda told Merrie about
awful Aunt Hildy, her plan
for the prize money, and how she
needed a ride *and* a lasso to win.

"Well," said Merrie, "I'll be your ride, so that leaves the rope."
Merrie nodded toward a sunbathing rattlesnake. "And
my little friend Slipper here is a big fan of lassoing."
The snake wiggled and slithered a *yeehaw!* "Just
have her home before sundown."

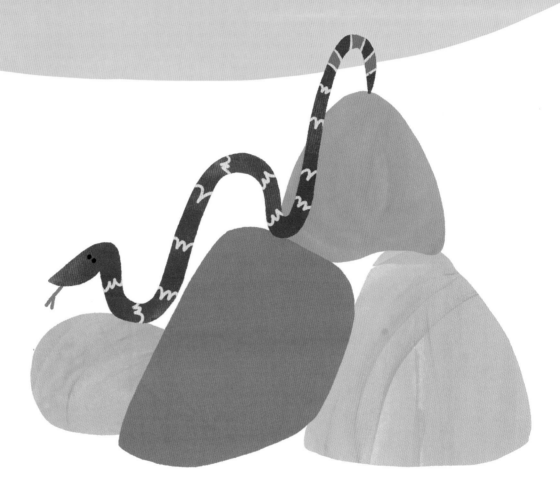

Cinda knew a snake without hot sun would get
grumpy, and a grumpy snake'd bite even if she liked
you. "Thank you both! But wait—I can't ride in this
junk!" Cinda whipped up a better outfit with some
burlap sacks, and they were on their way.

As the trio trotted onto the rancho, you could've heard a cactus needle drop. Who *was* this amazing burlap-wrapped contestant on a ginormous pig?

Cinda spotted The Rider sitting next to someone in a pile of pink ruffles. Must be Ella Del Reina.

"To the corral for the lasso challenge!" little Miss Ruffles called.

Cinda was expecting to lasso a longhorn. Instead, waddling around the corral was an iddy-biddy armadillo.

Suddenly Cinda was less worried 'bout winning, and more worried 'bout making sure that critter didn't get walloped by ropes.

"Ready, set, LASSO!"

Slipper whipped up that critter safely from the chaos, and Cinda won.

"Cheater!" screeched Hildy.

"Next challenge: Giddyap to that gulch and back!"

Merrie was faster than a snappy jackrabbit. But Cinda stopped to keep a few friends from getting stomped, so she came in second.

"A tie! But we can only have one winner!" said the pile of pink.

"What's our tiebreaker, Miss Ella?" Cinda asked, nervously looking at Slipper and the sinking sun.

"Oh! I'm Josefina. Ella's my sibling." She pointed to The Rider.

"Well, I'll be," said Cinda, beaming at the *real* Ella.

But Slipper was a-squirmin', reminding Cinda to hurry up and win. Living another day *with* Hildy and the boys *without* her critters would be worse than seven years of sunburn.

"Your final challenge is—"

Before The Rider could finish,
a tornado of a bull interrupted.

Everyone panicked—except Cinda. She
had a special way of calming cattle.

The bull was mesmerized.
The Rider was impressed.
The crowd was amazed.

And Slipper was getting cold.

Cinda didn't intend to end the day with venom, whether she'd broken the tie or not.

"We have to giddyap, Merrie!"

They skedaddled before the winner was announced.

As soon as Slipper was nestled under her rock,
Cinda burst into tears.

She'd been so close to getting her critters back! Now she had no prize, no pets, and no strength to stand another day with Hildy and the boys. Her heart hurt more than a hundred headaches.

A voice interrupted her drip-dropping tears.
"Say, you're the winner from today, ain't you?"
It was The Rider. Ella.

A screech sliced
through the sky.
"No! *He* was!" said Aunt
Hildy, pointing at one of
the boys, then the other.

"Then how about one of those *he's* shows me some boar-back riding?" Ella nodded toward Merrie. The boys suddenly had somewhere else to be.

"You know, you got a way with animals," said Ella, winking.

"Got a way with some people, too," said Cinda, winking right back.

"Wanna be our critter caretaker at the rancho?" said Ella.

"Depends," said Cinda. "Got room for my pets?"

"Plenty," said Ella.

"And do you like adventure?"

"Even more than jalapeño fritters," said Ella.

"Then let's giddyap," said Cinda,
smiling a new adventure in the face.